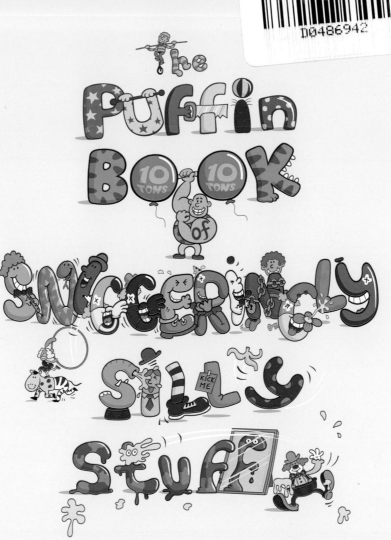

The Puffin Book of Sniggeringly Silly Stuff

The Puffin BOOK of SNIGGERINGLY SILLY STUFF

PUFFIN BOOKS

PUFFIN BOOKS

Published by the Penguin Group
Penguin Books Ltd, 27 Wrights Lane, London W8 5TZ, England
Penguin Putnam Inc., 375 Hudson Street, New York, New York 10014, USA
Penguin Books Australia Ltd, Ringwood, Victoria, Australia
Penguin Books Canada Ltd, 10 Alcorn Avenue, Toronto, Ontario, Canada M4V 3B2
Penguin Books India (P) Ltd, 11 Community Centre, Panchsheel Park, New Delhi – 110 017, India
Penguin Books (NZ) Ltd, Cnr Rosedale and Airborne Roads, Albany, Auckland, New Zealand
Penguin Books (South Africa) (Pty) Ltd, 5 Watkins Street, Denver Ext 4, Johannesburg 2094, South Africa

Penguin Books Ltd, Registered Offices: Harmondsworth, Middlesex, England

On the World Wide Web at: www.penguin.com

First published by Viking 2000
Published in Puffin Books 2001
3 5 7 9 10 8 6 4 2

Made and printed in Italy by Printer Trento Srl

British Library Cataloguing in Publication Data
A CIP catalogue record for this book is available from the British Library

ISBN 0-141-31161-4

CONTENTS
Family

School

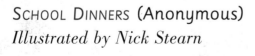

Monsters

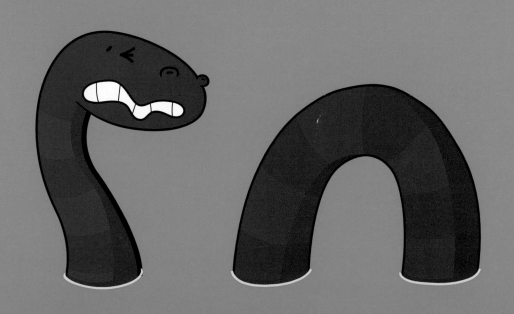

Food

Ghosts

Animals

MARGARET MAHY

Fair Exchange

Mr Salt had two sayings.

One was, Fair exchange is no robbery, and the other was, A man needs his sleep.

The seven Salt children were as sharp as needles and as bright as pins, and Mr Salt himself could sing songs of sad lovers or tell tales of mystery and adventure. However, his main hobby was sleeping. While he slept, the house got older and older and began to fall to pieces. Water came in like an invited guest, and so did Mr Salt's wild, hungry hens, who thought that the Salts' house was full of delicious food. Hens are usually timid, but Mr Salt's hens feared neither man nor beast.

Jeremy Salt, the oldest Salt child, complained to his father about the house tumbling down and the hens coming in, but all Mr Salt would say was, 'Only the house! Only the hens! Oh, let me sleep again,' and start a melodious but manly snoring that made Jeremy feel guilty about waking him in the first place.

However, one morning when the snoring started, Jeremy shook his father and woke him again.

'Is it the end of the world?' asked Mr Salt, opening eyes as blue as periwinkles for the second time that morning.

'No, Dad, no! Just listen! A window's come out and a door's fallen in and the hens are all over the kitchen. They've pecked the cat and the baby. Can't you build a chicken coop, Dad, so the hens will stay put?'

'Goodness me!' cried Mr Salt. 'If only your dead mother were alive. *There* was a woman who could have put a chicken coop up in a flash. Oh well, I've done a bit of building in my time. Bring me the hammer and bring me the nails and bring me some two-by-two.'

'What's two-by-two, Daddy?' asked one of the seven little Salts – a girl one.

'It's a size of wood, my dear, a very famous size, two inches this way and two inches that . . . it's what Noah built the ark out of.'

'The ark, Daddy?'

'Yes, my dear – haven't you heard the animals went in two by two too?'

The Salt children bought a little and borrowed a little and carried it to the other end of the garden. The hens watched them out of small yellow eyes, each hen standing on one leg with curiosity.

'Carry Dad down to the end of the section. Don't make him walk or he'll be tired out,' said Jeremy. The seven little Salts pushed and pulled Mr Salt's bed down to the other end of the garden. Mr Salt opened one eye and saw the hammer, saw the nails, saw the two-by-two.

'Get to work, my darlings,' he whispered. 'You can do it if you try. I'll give you a few clues.'

In between yawns, Mr Salt told his children where to saw and where to hammer and which end of the nail came first.

'Make it big,' he commanded. 'Those hens are used to the freedom of the hedge. I don't want them to be miserable.'

As the chicken coop grew bigger and bigger, the children

became more and more interested. They painted the door blue and the roof red. They put up window boxes full of wild flowers – yarrow, mayweed, plantain and pimpernel. They made a lovely, long chicken coop, with two-by-two and chicken wire. At last they were finished. Then the little Salts looked at the new henhouse and sighed.

'What a beautiful house!' they said to one another. 'Daddy, may we get our little chairs and sit in the house for a while before we put the hens in it?'

'A good idea,' Mr Salt

declared. 'Push my bed in too. I'm all worn out with mental activity. I'll have a little nap in the shade.'

Looking out from the chicken coop, the little Salts saw the world quite differently. From this end of the garden they could look between the hills and see the blue waters of the sea. As the sun set, the blue turned to gold and the hills were edged with scarlet.

'Daddy, may we bring down our big bed and the patchwork quilt and sleep in the henhouse all night?' asked the little Salts.

'Certainly, my dears,' replied Mr Salt, between breathing in and breathing out.

So the little Salts brought down their big bed and their patchwork quilt and slept all night in the new henhouse.

In the morning there were no hens to scratch on the doormat and peck at the floor. They were all up at the big house wondering where the Salt family had got to. And even when they found them, they couldn't get at them, because the chicken coop, made for keeping the hens in, was also very good at keeping them out, so the baby could eat her biscuit in peace without any fear that a hen might snatch it out of pure greed and malice.

'Oh, Father!' said the little Salts. 'Let the hens have our old

house and let us live in the nice new henhouse.'

'A good idea!' said Mr Salt. 'Fair exchange is no robbery. Besides, having got this far, I doubt if I have the strength to move back again. After all, a man does need his sleep, you know.'

So the Salt family lived in the henhouse with the blue door and the hens lived in the Salts' old house. Pieces kept on dropping off the old house and the view wasn't very good, but the hens didn't mind and laid just as many eggs as if they too could watch the sea turn golden in the evening, or silver by the light of the moon.

SPIKE MILLIGAN
Granny

Through every nook and every cranny
The wind blew in on poor old Granny;
Around her knees, into each ear
(And up her nose as well, I fear).

All through the night the wind grew worse,
It nearly made the vicar curse.
The top had fallen off the steeple
Just missing him (and other people).

It blew on man; it blew on beast.
It blew on nun; it blew on priest.
It blew the wig off Auntie Fanny –
But most of all, it blew on Granny!

MICHAEL ROSEN

Tricks

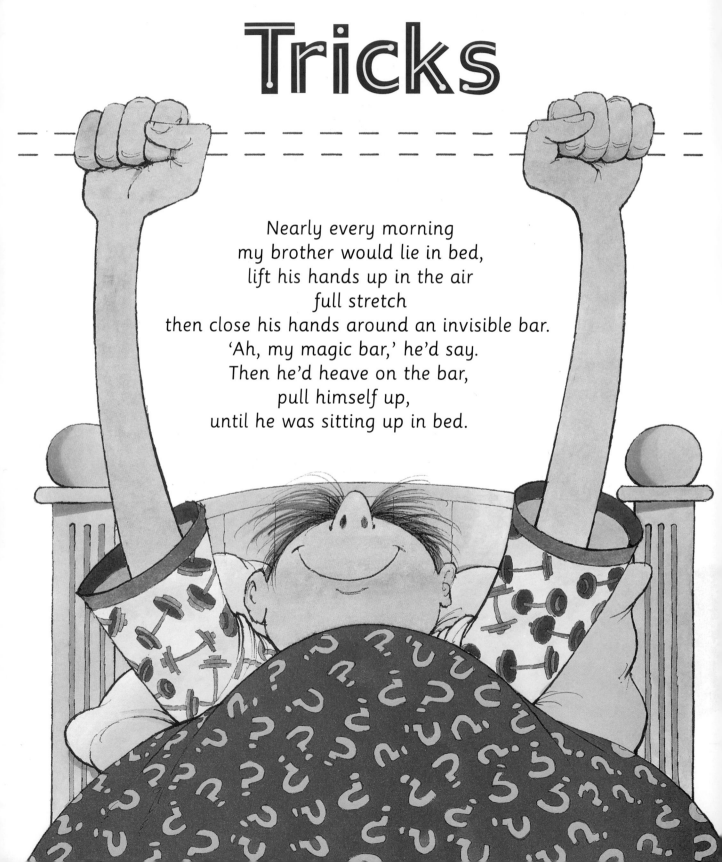

Nearly every morning
my brother would lie in bed,
lift his hands up in the air
full stretch
then close his hands around an invisible bar.
'Ah, my magic bar,' he'd say.
Then he'd heave on the bar,
pull himself up,
until he was sitting up in bed.

Then he'd get up.
I said,
'You haven't got a magic bar above your bed.'
'I have,' he said.
'You haven't,' I said.
'Don't believe me then,' he said.
'I won't – don't worry,' I said.
'It doesn't make any difference to me
if you do or you don't,' he said,
and went out of the room.

'Magic bar!' I said.
'Mad. He hasn't got a magic bar.'
I made sure he'd gone downstairs,
then I walked over to his bed
and waved my hand about in the air
above his pillow.
'I knew it,' I said to myself.
'Didn't fool me for a moment.'

Daughter: My teacher does bird impressions.

Mother: What do you mean?

Daughter: She watches me like a hawk!

'My grandfather has a wooden leg.'
'That's nothing, my uncle has a pine chest!'

Dad: What position are you playing in the school football team?

Son: The coach says I'm the main drawback!

'I'm afraid your son has swallowed a coin.'

'That's all right, it was his lunch money!'

'Mummy, I banged my head!'
'Come here and I'll hiss it better.'

'Mum, can I try on that dress in the window?'

'I think you'd better use the changing room, dear.'

SALE! 50% off

RICHARD EDWARDS

Lost and Found

I was worrying over some homework
When my grandad walked into the room
And sat wearily down with a grunt and a frown
And a face full of sorrow and gloom.

'I've lost it, I've lost it,' he muttered,
'And it's very important to me.'
'Lost what?' I replied. 'I've forgotten,' he sighed.
'But it's something beginning with T.'

'A toffee, perhaps,' I suggested,
'Or a teapot or even your tie,
Or some toast or a thread . . .'
but he shook his grey head
As a tear trickled out of one eye.

12

'A **tuba**,' I said, 'or some **treacle**,
Or a **toggle** to sew on your mac,
Or a **tray** or a ticket, a **tree** or a thicket,
A thistle, a taper, a **tack**.'

But Grandad looked blank. 'Well, some **tweezers**,
Or a **theory**,' I said, 'or a **tooth**,
Or a **tap** or a till or a **thought** or a thrill
Or your **trousers**, a trestle, the **truth**.'

'It's none of those things,' grumbled Grandad.
'A toy **trumpet**,' I offered, 'a **trowel**,
Or a **trout**, a tureen, an antique **tambourine**,
A **toboggan**, a tortoise, a trowel . . .'

Then suddenly Grandad's scowl vanished.
'I've remembered!' he cried with a shout.
'It's my **temper**, you brat, so come here and

take that!'

And he boxed both my ears and went out.

MARGARET PORTER

Are You Receiving Me?

'How's Auntie? Feeling the cold?'
'Old? You don't think I'm old?
I'm a young eighty-nine
And most of the time
I'm like a spring lamb in the fold!'

'It's good that you're hale and hearty.'
'Party? Who's having a party?
Not quite my thing,
Hope it goes with a swing,
But I find all your friends
a bit arty!'

'We thought we'd come for the day.'

'Stay? You can't come and stay.
I've scrapped the spare bed,
Come for supper instead,
I'm sure you remember the way.'

'I'll bring you a bunch of flowers.'

'Showers? Did you say showers?
For this time of year
It's incredibly clear;
No sign of a cloud for some hours!'

'Oh and Jo has passed her exam.'

'Pram? You've bought a new pram?
That's wonderful news,
You all know my views!
I can't say how delighted I am!'

'Goodbye, then – and love to the cat!'

'Flat? I don't live in a flat!
(My niece is devoted,
But lately I've noted
She's developed this odd line in chat!)'

MICK GOWAR

Christmas Thank Yous

Dear Auntie
Oh, what a nice jumper
I've always adored powder blue
and fancy you thinking of
orange and pink
for the stripes
how clever of you

Dear Uncle
The soap is terrific
So useful
and such a kind thought and
how did you guess that
I'd just used the last of
the soap that last Christmas brought

FAMiLY JOKES

Why wouldn't the piglets listen to their father?
He was an awful old boar.

'My granny has teeth like stars.'
'Really?'
'Yes – they come out at night!'

Where was Grandma when the lights went out? In the dark.

'My father gets a warm reception wherever he goes.'

'He must be very popular.'

'No, he's a fireman.'

What did the baby hedgehog say when it bumped into a cactus?

'Is that you, Mum?'

Why was the Egyptian boy worried?

Because his daddy was a mummy.

KIT WRIGHT
What Went Wrong at my Sister's Wedding

The bridegroom was supposed
To kiss the bride,
Not kick 'er

And

He shouldn't have kissed
The vicar

And

They should have thrown
Confetti,

Not
Spaghetti.

JAN MARK

The One That Got Away

'And what have we to remember to bring tomorrow?' Mrs Cooper
asked, at half past three. Malcolm, sitting near the back,
wondered why she said 'we'. *She* wasn't going to bring anything.

'Something interesting, Mrs Cooper,' said everyone else, all
together.

'And what are we going to do then?'

'Stand up and talk about it, Mrs Cooper.'

'So don't forget. All right. Chairs on tables. Goodbye, Class Four.'

'Goodbye, Mrs Cooper. Goodbye everybody.'

It all came out ever so slow, like saying prayers in assembly. 'Amen,' said Malcolm, very quietly. Class Four put its chairs on the tables, collected its coats and went home, talking about all the interesting things it would bring into school tomorrow.

Malcolm walked by himself. Mrs Cooper had first told them to find something interesting on Monday. Now it was Thursday and still he had not come up with any bright ideas. There were plenty of things that he found interesting, but the trouble was, they never seemed to interest anyone else. Last time this had happened he had brought along his favourite stone and shown it to the class.

'Very nice, Malcolm,' Mrs Cooper had said. 'Now tell us what's interesting about it.' He hadn't know what to say. Surely anyone looking at the stone could see how interesting it was.

Mary was going to bring her gerbil. James, Sarah and William had loudly discussed rare shells and fossils, and the only spider in the world with five legs.

'It can't be a spider then,' said David, who was eavesdropping.

'It had an accident,' William said.

Isobel intended to bring her pocket calculator and show them how it could write her name by punching in 738051 and turning it upside down. She did this every time, but it still looked interesting.

Malcolm could think of nothing.

When he reached home, he went up to his bedroom and looked at the shelf where he kept important things; his twig that looked like a stick insect, his marble that looked like a glass eye, the penny

with a hole in it and the Siamese-twin jelly-babies, one red, one green and stuck together, back to back. He noticed that they were now stuck to the shelf too. His stone had once been there as well, but after Class Four had said it was boring he had put it back in the garden. He still went to see it sometimes.

What he really needed was something that could move about, like Mary's gerbil or William's five-legged spider. He sat down on his bed and began to think.

On Friday, after assembly, Class Four began to be interesting. Mary kicked off with the gerbil that whirred round its cage like a hairy balloon with the air escaping. Then they saw William's

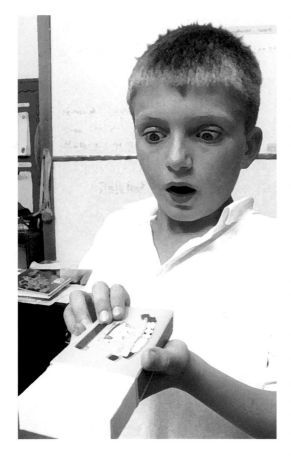

lame spider, James's fossil, Jason's collection of snail shells stuck one on top of the other like the leaning tower of Pisa, and David's bottled conkers that he had kept in an air-tight jar for three years. They were still as glossy as new shoes.

Then it was Malcolm's turn. He went up to the front and held out a matchbox. He had chosen it very carefully. It was the kind with the same label top and bottom so that when you opened it you could never be sure that it was the right way up and all the matches fell out. Malcolm opened it upside down and jumped. Mrs Cooper jumped too. Malcolm threw himself down on hands and knees and looked under her desk.

'What's the matter?' Mrs Cooper said.

'It's fallen out!' Malcolm cried.

'What is it?' Mrs Cooper said, edging away.

'I don't know – it's got six legs and sharp knees . . . and sort of frilly ginger eyebrows on stalks –' He pounced. 'There it goes.'

'Where?'

'Missed it,' said Malcolm. 'It's running under your chair, Mary.'

Mary squeaked and climbed on to the table because she thought that was the right way to behave when creepy-crawlies were about.

'I see it!' Jason yelled, and jumped up and down. David threw a book in the direction that Jason was pointing and James began beating the floor with a rolled-up comic.

'I got it – I killed it,' he shouted.

'It's crawling up the curtains,' Sarah said and Mrs Cooper, who was standing by the curtains, moved rapidly away from them.

'It's over by the door,' Mary shrieked, and several people ran to head it off. Chairs were overturned.

Malcolm stood by Mrs Cooper's desk with his matchbox. His contribution was definitely the most interesting thing that anyone had seen that morning. He was only sorry that he hadn't seen it himself.

BRIAN PATTEN

Gust Becos I Cud Not Spel

Gust becos I cud not spel
It did not mean I was daft
When the boys in school red my riting
Some of them laffed

But now I am the dictater
They have to rite like me
Utherwise they cannot pas
Ther GCSE

Some of the girls were OK
But those who laffed a lot
Have al bean rownded up
And hav recintly bean shot

The teecher who corrected my speling
As not been shot at al
But four the last fifteen howers
As bean standing up against a wal

He has to stand ther until he can spel
Figgymisgrugifooniyn the rite way
I think he will stand ther for ever
I just inventid it today

TEACHER:
Where do you find
the Andes?

GIRL:
At the end
of your wristies.

What did
one maths
book say
to the other?

I've got
problems.

$2x+4$
-3
$x/2-4+3$

There once was a teacher from Leeds
Who swallowed a packet of seeds.
In less than an hour
Her nose was a flower
And her hair was a
bundle of weeds.

PAUL COOKSON

My Dad the Headmaster

My dad the headmaster knows every single rule
and when he is at home he thinks that he's at school.
He rings the bell each morning and I'd better not be late
so I'm washed and down for breakfast at exactly ten to eight.

He stands and takes the register, checks my shirt and tie,
then he says 'Good morning' and I have to reply
'Gerd mor-ning Far-ther' in that monotone drone,
then hear his assembly in our very own home.

He has a list of rules that are pasted on each door:
No Spitting. **No** Chewing. **No** Litter on the Floor.
No Music. **No** Jewellery. **No** Make-up. **No** Telly.
No Making Rude Noises Especially If They're
Smelly.

No Videos. **No** Football.
No Coloured Socks Or Laces.
No Trainers. **No** Jeans. **No** Smiling Faces.
No Sticking Bubble Gum in Your Sister's Hair.
No Wiping Bogies Down the Side of the Chair.

He has a list of sayings for all types of occasion
And a set of phrases for every situation:
'Don't run down the stairs. Speak when spoken to.
Put your hand up first if you want to use the loo.'

'I don't mind how long I wait. Listen when I'm speaking.
No one leaves the table until we've finished eating.
Don't interrupt and don't answer back.
Don't do this and don't do that.

Yes my dad the headmaster knows every single rule
and when he is at home he thinks that he's at school.
But I am not the only one who does what he is told.
Dad never complains if his dinner is cold.

He's ever so polite when my mother is around
and mumbles 'Yes, my dear' while looking at the ground.
Her foghorn commands, they really drive him crazy.
Dad's scared stiff of Mum cos she's a dinner lady!

JOHN AGARD

Laughter Rap in Plastic Town

One day as I was passing through plastic town
I happened to pass a school playground
yet I couldn't hear one laughing sound.

Can you imagine a school playground
and not a single laughing sound?
But that's how it was in plastic town.

For though they were playing as children play,
plastic children do so in a most unusual way.
Not one was laughing, not one I say.

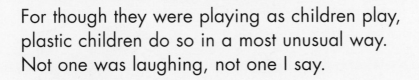

Every move they made was made of plastic
it was sad to see children so robotic.
They could do with a touch of my laughing magic.

So I reached for my hip-hop cap
got into my egg-leg tap
broke into my laughing rap.

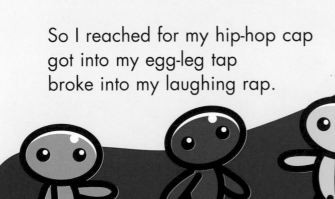

Children, children of plastic town
it makes me sad to see you frown.
Cracking up with laughter is the thing to do,
cracking up with laughter makes you feel brand-new.
So give me a crick, give me a crack,
just throw yourself into the laughing act.

I promise my magic will bring you right back.

TREVOR HARVEY

The Painting Lesson

'What's THAT, dear?'
Asked the new teacher.
'It's Mummy,'
I replied.
'But mums aren't green and orange!
You really haven't TRIED.
You don't just paint SPLODGES;
You're old enough to know
You need to THINK before you work.
Now – have another go.'

She helped me draw two arms and legs,
A face with sickly smile,
A rounded body, dark brown hair,
A hat – and in a while
She stood back, with her face bright pink:
'That's SO much better, don't you think?'

But she turned white
At ten to three
When an orange-green blob
Collected me.

'Hi, Mum!'

34

COLIN WEST

In One Ear and Out the Other

When Miss Tibbs talks
To my dear brother,
It goes in one ear
And out the other.
And when she shouts,
He seldom hears,
The words just whistle
Through his ears.

His ears are big
(You must've seen them),
But he's got nothing
In between them.
The truth, Miss Tibbs,
Is hard to face.
His head is full
Of empty space.

35

SCHOOL JOKES

What did the teacher **bee** say to the naughty **bee**? 'Be**hive** yourself'.

Why did the teacher wear dark glasses? Because her class was so **bright**.

What is the **rudest** food we have at school? Sausages, because they **spit**.

TEACHER: Joe, your homework seems to be in your father's handwriting.
JOE: Yes, Miss, I used his pen.

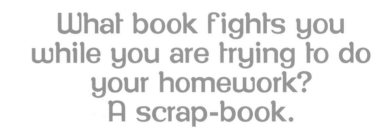

What book fights you while you are trying to do your homework?
A scrap-book.

Why was the teacher **cross-eyed**?
He couldn't control his **pupils**!

37

ANONYMOUS

Music Tutor

A tutor who taught on the flute,
Tried to teach two young tooters to toot;
Said the two to the tutor:
'Is it harder to toot, or
To tutor two tooters to toot?'

ANONYMOUS

SCHOOL DINNERS

If you stay for school dinners
Better throw them aside;
A lot of kids didn't,
A lot of kids died.

The meat is made of iron,
The spuds are made of steel;
And if that don't get you
the afters will!

MARJORIE STANNARD

Thomas and the Monster

Thomas put on his wellies and his lucky woollen hat and walked up the garden path.

'I see you've got your lucky hat on,' remarked Snoodles the tortoise, who was just waking up from a nap on the grass. 'Are you going somewhere special?'

'Just looking for Monsters,' said Thomas. 'There might be one at the bottom, where the stream is.'

'Well, don't shout for me if you find one,' said Snoodles sleepily. 'I'm just going to have another little sleep in the rhubarb patch.'

Thomas walked on, under the cherry trees, until he came to the little summer house by the stream. It was very quiet down here.

The stream was half dried up and only made a soft murmur as it ran, and the birds only twittered now and then because they were resting in green branches away from the hot sun.

He walked round the summer house and looked in through its small dusty window. He couldn't see very well because the dust was quite thick, so he rubbed the glass with his lucky woollen hat.

Then he looked again. Inside was a wooden table with two chairs. On the table lay a heap of red cherries. And sitting on one of the chairs was a Monster.

Thomas knew he was a Monster because his hair was green and very short, like fur, and he had two horns sticking out – one above each ear.

Thomas put on his lucky hat again and opened the door.

'Hello,' he said, 'are you a Monster?'

The Monster looked rather frightened. 'I hope you don't mind me being here,' he said nervously, in a kind of choky voice, as though he had a sore throat. 'I couldn't find anywhere else to sleep. And I had a few cherries.'

Thomas sat down on the other chair. 'I don't mind at all,' he said. And he gave the Monster a handful of cherries and took some himself.

'I was on my way back to the mountains,' the Monster explained, putting some cherry-stones neatly in a row, 'when somehow I took a wrong turning. I got mixed up with motorways and railway stations and yards full of buses. Nobody saw me because I'm rather good at dodging underneath things. In the end I found myself in your garden. I am quite worn out. So I had a drink of stream-water and a few cherries, and came in here.'

'You can stay as long as you want,' said Thomas kindly. 'Which mountains are you going to?'

'This year,' said the Monster, 'I'm going to Wales. My uncle told me of a nice dry cave by a lake that will just suit me.'

'I think my dad's got a map of England and Wales,' said

Thomas, looking excited. 'Wait here for me.' And he ran up the path into the house. Thomas went into the kitchen and asked Mum if he could borrow the map for a little while. Mum got it out of the bureau drawer for him.

'Be careful with it,' said Mum, 'and put it back in the drawer when you've finished.' Thomas carried the map down to the garden and spread it out on the table so that the Monster could see it properly.

After a little while the Monster said happily, 'Now I see where I went wrong! Do you mind if I take a few cherries in my pocket? Thank you very much. I'll be on my way now. And if ever you come to that lake in North Wales I showed you, be sure to look me up. My relations will

all be very pleased to meet you. I suppose,' he added, blinking his rather beautiful green eyes, 'I suppose you wouldn't let me try your hat on before I go?'

Thomas was a little doubtful if it would fit him, as he had a couple of horns to manage; but when Thomas passed it over, he put it on his head quite easily, letting the horns poke through on each side.

'It *does* feel nice and warm,' said the Monster, giving a sort of sigh. And he was just going to take it off when Thomas said suddenly, 'No, you keep it. It's a lucky hat, so I'm sure you'll get to Wales all right.'

The Monster beamed. 'I'll be off then. Goodbye!'

And he hurried through the door and disappeared among the bushes.

Thomas folded the map up carefully. Then he looked at the

Monster's cherry-stones lying in a neat row.

'I'll keep them,' said Thomas to himself. 'Then nobody can say I haven't really seen a Monster.'

When he got back to the kitchen Mum said, 'Where's your lucky hat?'

'I've lent it to a Monster,' said Thomas.

'Well,' said Mum, 'it was time you had a new one, anyway.'

And that very evening she started to knit him a new one.

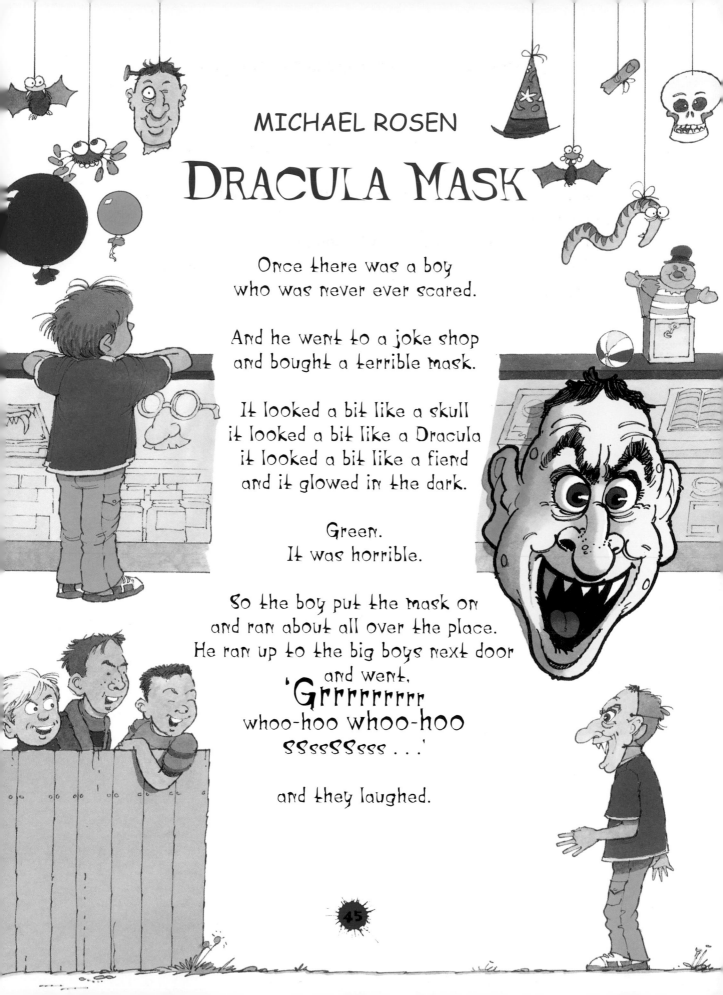

MICHAEL ROSEN

DRACULA MASK

Once there was a boy
who was never ever scared.

And he went to a joke shop
and bought a terrible mask.

It looked a bit like a skull
it looked a bit like a Dracula
it looked a bit like a fiend
and it glowed in the dark.

Green.
It was horrible.

So the boy put the mask on
and ran about all over the place.
He ran up to the big boys next door
and went,
'Grrrrrrrrr
whoo-hoo whoo-hoo
sssssssss . . .'

and they laughed.

So he went to the park
and there were some ducks
and so he went,
'Grrrrrrrrr
whoo-hoo whoo-hoo
sssssSsss . . .'

and the ducks swam slowly round and round and round
looking for bits of bread.

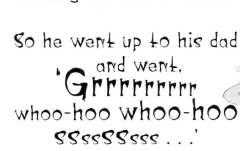

So he went up to his dad
and went,
'Grrrrrrrrr
whoo-hoo whoo-hoo
sssssSsss . . .'

and his dad looked at him and said,
'We should have brought some bread for the ducks.'

So he rushed up to
a big
woolly
mongrel
dog

and went,
'Grrrrrrrrr
whoo-hoo whoo-hoo whoo-hoo
sssssSsss . . .'

and the dog went,
'Wuff wuff wuff,'
very loudly
and rushed at that
green Dracula skull fiend
and tried to bite its head off.

And the green Dracula skull fiend ran
and the green Dracula skull fiend screamed,
it went,
'Daddy Daddy Daddy
help me help me help me.'

So,
it can be very very scary
trying to make
a big woolly mongrel dog
very very scared . . .

LEWIS CARROLL

JABBERWOCKY

'Twas brillig, and the slithy toves
Did gyre and gimble in the wabe;
All mimsy were the borogroves,
And the mome raths outgrabe.

'Beware the Jabberwock, my son!
The jaws that bite, the claws that catch!
Beware the Jubjub bird, and shun
The frumious Bandersnatch!'

He took his vorpal sword in hand:
Long time the manxome foe he sought –
So rested he by the Tumtum tree,
And stood awhile in thought.

And, as in uffish thought he stood,
The Jabberwock, with eyes of flame,
Came whiffling through the tulgy wood,
And burbled as it came!

One, two! One, two! And through and through
The vorpal blade went snicker-snack!
He left it dead, and with its head
He went galumphing back.

'And hast thou slain the Jabberwock?
Come to my arms, my beamish boy!
O frabjous day! Callooh! Callay!'
He chortled in his joy.

'Twas brillig and the slithy toves
Did gyre and gimble in the wabe;
All mimsy were the borogroves,
And the mome raths outgrabe.

JAMES REEVES

THE KWACKAGEE

Back in the bleak and blurry days
When all was murk and mystery -
That is (if I may mint a phrase)
Before the dawn of history,
Professors think there used to be,
Not far from Waikee-waike,
A monster called the Kwackagee,
A sort of flying snake.

This animile, they all agree,
Was forty feet in length,
Would spiral up the tallest tree
And then with all his strength
Propel himself with sinuous grace
And undulation muscular
To find another feeding-place
In some far vale crepuscular.

Expert opinions are two
About his mode of travel:
Professor Grommit holds one view:
The other, Doctor Gravvle.
Grommit believes he could give off
Some kind of speed-emulsion:
The Doctor, ever prone to scoff,
Postulates jet-propulsion.

In prehistoric Waikee-waike,
The men (if men there were),
Would they in breathless terror quake
To hear that rattling whirr
As flew the monster through the sky?
Or would they brave the foe
With missile and with battle-cry?
The experts do not know.

MONSTER JOKES

Young monster: That girl just rolled her eyes at me.

Mummy monster: Well roll them back, she might need them.

What did the monster say when he saw a man sleeping?

'Ah, breakfast in bed!'

What did the grape say when the monster stood on it?

Nothing, it just gave a little wine.

What did the monster eat after its teeth were pulled out? The dentist

Which monster is a friend of the three bears? Ghouldilocks.

What does a vegetarian monster eat? Swedes.

ROALD DAHL
The Tummy Beast

One afternoon I said to Mummy,
'Who is this person in my tummy?
He must be small and very thin
Or how could he have gotten in?'
My mother said from where she sat,
'It isn't nice to talk like that.'
'It's true!' I cried. 'I swear it, Mummy!
There *is* a person in my tummy!
He talks to me at night in bed,
He's always asking to be fed,
Throughout the day, he screams at me,
Demanding sugar buns for tea.
He tells me it is not a sin
To go and raid the biscuit tin.
I know quite well it's awfully wrong
To guzzle food the whole day long,
But really I can't help it, Mummy,
Not with this person in my tummy.'

'You horrid child!' my mother cried.
'Admit it right away, you've lied!
You're simply trying to produce
A silly asinine excuse!

You are the greedy
guzzling brat!
And that is why
you're always fat!'
I tried once more,
'*Believe me*, Mummy,
There *is* a person in my tummy.'
'I've had enough!' my mother said,
'You'd better go at once to bed!'
Just then, a nicely timed event
Delivered me from punishment.
Deep in my tummy something stirred,
And then an awful noise was heard,
A snorting grumbling grunting sound
That made my tummy jump around.
My darling mother nearly died,

'My goodness, what was that?' she cried.
At once, the tummy voice came through,
It shouted, 'Hey there! Listen you!
I'm getting hungry! I want eats!
I want lots of chocs and sweets!
Get me half a pound of nuts!
Look snappy or I'll twist your guts!'
'That's him!' I cried. *'He's in my tummy!*
So now do you believe me, Mummy?'
But Mummy answered nothing more,
For she had fainted
on the floor.

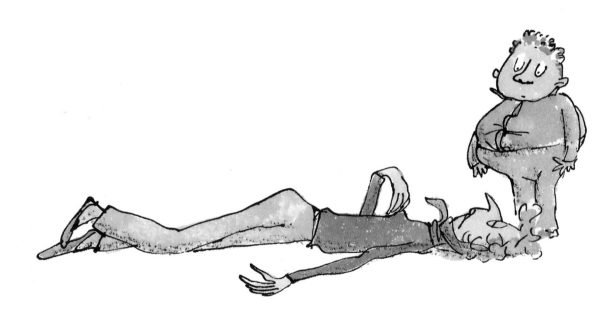

ANN CAMERON

The Pudding Like a Night on the Sea

'I'm going to make
something special for your
mother,' my father said.

My mother was out
shopping. My father was
in the kitchen looking at
the pots and the pans and the jars of this and that.

'What are you going to make?' I said.

'A pudding,' he said.

My father is a big man with wild black hair. When he laughs,
the sun laughs in the window-panes. When he thinks, you can
almost see his thoughts sitting on all the tables and chairs. When
he is angry, me and my little brother Huey shiver to the bottom of
our shoes.

'What kind of pudding will you make?' Huey said.

'A wonderful pudding,' my father said. 'It will taste like a
whole raft of lemons. It will taste like a night on the sea.'

Then he took down a knife and sliced five lemons in half. He

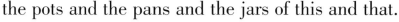

squeezed the first one. Juice squirted in my eye.

'Stand back!' he said, and squeezed again. The seeds flew out on the floor. 'Pick up those seeds, Huey!' he said.

Huey took the broom and swept them up.

My father cracked some eggs and put the yolks in a pan and the whites in a bowl. He rolled up his sleeves and pushed back his hair and beat up the yolks. 'Sugar, Julian!' he said, and I poured in the sugar.

He went on beating. Then he put in lemon juice and cream and set the pan on the stove. The pudding bubbled and he stirred it fast. Cream splashed on the stove.

'Wipe that up, Huey! he said.

Huey did.

It was hot by the stove. My father loosened his collar and pushed at his sleeves. The stuff in the pan was getting thicker and thicker. He held the beater up high in the air. 'Just right!' he said, and sniffed in the smell of the pudding.

He whipped the egg whites and mixed them into the pudding. The pudding looked softer and lighter than air.

'Done!' he said. He washed all the pots, splashing water on the floor, and wiped the counter so fast his hair made circles around his head.

'Perfect!' he said. 'Now I'm going to

take a nap. If something important happens, bother me. If nothing important happens, don't bother me. And – the pudding is for your mother. Leave the pudding alone!'

He went to the living room and was asleep in a minute, sitting straight up in his chair.

Huey and I guarded the pudding.

'Oh, it's a wonderful pudding,' Huey said.

'With waves on the top like the ocean,' I said.

'I wonder how it tastes,' Huey said.

'Leave the pudding alone,' I said.

'If I just put my finger in – there – I'll know how it tastes,' Huey said.

And he did it.

'You did it!' I said. 'How does it taste?'

'It tastes like a whole raft of lemons,' he said. 'It tastes like a night on the sea.'

'You've made a hole in the pudding!' I said. 'But since you did it, I'll have a taste.'

And it tasted like a whole night of lemons. It tasted like floating at sea.

'It's such a big pudding,' Huey said. 'It can't hurt to have a little more.'

'Since you took more, I'll have more,' I said.

'That was a bigger lick than I took!' Huey said. 'I'm going to have more again.'

'Whoops!' I said.

'You put in your whole hand!' Huey said. 'Look at the pudding you spilled on the floor!'

'I am going to clean it up,' I said. And I took the rag from the sink.

'That's not really clean,' Huey said.

'It's the best I can do,' I said.

'Look at the pudding!' Huey said.

It looked like craters on the moon. 'We have to smooth this over,' I said. 'So it looks the way it did before! Let's get spoons.'

And we evened the top of the pudding with spoons, and while we evened it, we ate some more.

'There isn't much left,' I said.

'We were supposed to leave the pudding alone,' Huey said.

'We'd better get away from here,' I said. We ran into our bedroom and crawled under the bed. After a long time we heard my father's voice.

'Come into the kitchen, dear,' he said. 'I have something for you.'

'Why, what is it?' my mother said, out in the kitchen.

Under the bed, Huey and I pressed ourselves to the wall.

'Look,' said my father, out in the kitchen. 'A wonderful pudding.'

'Where is the pudding?' my mother said.

'WHERE ARE YOU BOYS?' my father said. His voice went through every crack and corner of the house.

We felt like two leaves in a storm.

'WHERE ARE YOU? I SAID!' My father's voice was booming.

Huey whispered to me, 'I'm scared'.

We heard my father walking slowly through the rooms.

'Huey!' he called. 'Julian!'

We could see his feet. He was coming into our room.

He lifted the bedspread. There was his face, and his eyes like black lighting. He grabbed us by the legs and pulled.

'STAND UP!' he said.

We stood.

'What do you have to tell me?' he said.

'We went outside,' Huey said, 'and when we came back, the pudding was gone!'

'Then why were you hiding under the bed?' my father said.

We didn't say anything. We looked at the floor.

'I can tell you one thing,' he said. 'There is going to be some beating here now! There is going to be some whipping!'

The curtains at the window were shaking. Huey was holding my hand.

'Go into the kitchen!' my father said. 'Right now!'

We went into the kitchen.

'Come here, Huey!' my father said.

Huey walked towards him, his hands behind his back.

'See these eggs?' my father said. He cracked them and put the yolks in a pan and set the pan on the counter. He stood a chair by the counter. 'Stand up here,' he said to Huey.

Huey stood on the chair by the counter.

'Now it's time for your beating!' my father said.

Huey started to cry. His tears fell in with the egg yolks.

'Take this!' my father said. My father handed him the egg beater. 'Now beat those eggs,' he said. 'I want this to be a good beating!'

'Oh!' Huey said. He stopped crying. And he beat the egg yolks.

'Now you, Julian, stand here!' my father said.

I stood on a chair by the table.

'I hope you're ready for your whipping!'

I didn't answer. I was afraid to say yes or no.

'Here!' he said, and he set the egg whites in front of me.

'I want these whipped and whipped well!'

'Yes, sir!' I said, and started whipping.

My father watched us. My mother came into the kitchen and watched us.

After a while Huey said, 'This is hard work.'

'That's too bad,' my father said. 'Your beating's not done!' And he added sugar and cream and lemon juice to Huey's pan and put the pan on the stove. And Huey went on beating.

'My arm hurts from whipping,' I said.

'That's too bad,' my father said. 'Your whipping's not done.'

So I whipped and whipped, and Huey beat and beat.

'Hold that beater in the air, Huey!' my father said.

Huey held it in the air.

'See!' my father said. 'A good pudding stays on the beater. It's thick enough now. Your beating's done.' Then he turned to me. 'Let's see those egg whites, Julian!' he said. They were puffed up and fluffy. 'Congratulations, Julian!' he said. 'Your whipping's done.'

He mixed the egg whites into the pudding himself. Then he passed the pudding to my mother.

'A wonderful pudding,' she said. 'Would you like some, boys?'

'No thank you,' we said.

She picked up a spoon. 'Why, this tastes like a whole raft of lemons,' she said. 'This tastes like a night on the sea.'

S-J MORTIMER   Golden Syrup

I'd like a bag of toenails, or a long-forgotten prune, but give me golden syrup, and I'd lick it from the spoon.

MARGARET MAHY

Unexpected Summer Soup

I drank some soup this afternoon,
  And what do you think I found in my spoon?
    Onions and Peas!
      Of course I didn't mind.
        It's what you'd expect to find.

    I drank some soup this afternoon.
      And what do you think I found in my spoon?
    Onions and Peas,
  A Hive of Bees . . .
    Oh, what a surprise!
      I couldn't believe my eyes.

      I drank some soup this afternoon,
        And what do you think I found in my spoon?
          Onions and Peas,
            A Hive of Bees,
              A Crown, a Carrot . . .
        Oh, shivers and shocks!
        I nearly jumped out of my socks.

      I drank some soup this afternoon,
        And what do you think I found in my spoon?
    Onions and Peas,

A Hive of Bees,
A Crown, a Carrot,
A Patchwork Parrot . . .
A-ghast, a-gape, a-gog,
I nearly stood on the dog.

I drank some soup this afternoon,
And what do you think I found in my spoon?
Onions and Peas,
A Hive of Bees,
A Crown, a Carrot,
A Patchwork Parrot,
A Sprig of Sage . . .
I didn't choose to object,
It's what you might expect.

I drank some soup this afternoon,
And what do you think I found in my spoon?
Onions and Peas,
A Hive of Bees,
A Crown, a Carrot,
A Patchwork Parrot,
A Sprig of Sage,

A Frog in a Cage . . .
What do you say to that?
It certainly scared the cat.

I drank some soup this afternoon.
     And what do you think I found in my spoon?
          Onions and Peas,
     A Hive of Bees,
A Crown, a Carrot,
     A Patchwork Parrot,
          A Sprig of Sage,
A Frog in a Cage,
A Witch's Shoe . . .
     Taken unaware,
          I tumbled off my chair.

I drank some soup this afternoon,
And what do you think I found in my spoon?
Onions and Peas,
     A Hive of Bees,
          A Crown, a Carrot,
               A Patchwork Parrot,
          A Sprig of Sage,

A Frog in a Cage,
　　A Witch's Shoe,
　　　　And a Mermaid too
　　　　　　Who sang a song so sweet and shrill
　　　　That the summery day outside stood still.

I asked my mother where she sat,
　　'How do you make a soup like that?'
　　　　'You have to gather, you have to guard
　　　　　　Things odd and even, striped and starred,
　　　　　　　　All the dark things, all the light,
　　　　　　That come to your door by day or night,
　　　　　　　　It isn't easy at all, my dear,
　　　　　　But I'll make it again another year,
　　　With . . .
　　　　Onions and Peas,
　　　　　　A Hive of Bees,
　　　　　　　　A Crown, a Carrot,
　　　　　　　　　　A Patchwork Parrot,
　　　　　　　　A Sprig of Sage,
　　　　　　A Frog in a Cage,
　　　　A Witch's Shoe,
　　　And a Mermaid too . . .
　　A Song, a Story, and anything more
That a summer wind brings to my door.

Why are **cooks** bullies?

They **whip** the cream and **beat** the eggs.

Knock, knock!
Who's there?
Egburt.
Egburt who?
Egg but no **bacon**.

What's yellow and **dangerous**?

Shark-infested **custard**.

What flies and wobbles?
A jellycopter.

What's **bad-tempered** and goes with **custard**?
Apple grumble.

What **cake** gives you an electric **shock**?
A **current bun.**

VERNON SCANNELL

Auntie Meg's Cookery Book

Tom liked his Auntie Meg a lot,
But even he confessed
She could not cook at all although
She *thought* she was the best.

She was a sport. She did not pry
Or lecture Tom or nag;
He loved to go and stay with her
Except for that big snag:

She was the worst cook in the world
And *thought* she was the best;
When she spent hours preparing cakes
He had to act impressed.

But worse, he had to *eat* the things;
Her rock cakes were no joke;
Not quite as hard as rock perhaps,
More like well-seasoned oak.

She often made a dumpling stew.
Today, Tom still recalls
Those dreaded objects in the pot
Like little cannonballs.

Her rice was gritty, porridge burnt;
You could have used her steak
For soling shoes, and one dropped bun
Once made the whole house shake.

The only way to dodge those meals
Was find some other craze
So interesting it would take up
All of her waking days.

So Tom persuaded her to write
A book. 'What kind?' she said.
'About what most appeals to you,
Pleasing heart and head.'

'A cookery book!' she cried. 'Oh yes!'
As lively as a kitten.
'Dear Tom, I'll write the very best
That anyone has written.'

And that's exactly what she did,
Scribbling day and night.
They had their meals in restaurants
To Tom's concealed delight.

At last her masterpiece appeared,
And she at once became
An expert in the cooking arts
With quickly spreading fame.

A star of radio and screen
Was dear old Auntie Meg,
And only Tom, her nephew, knew
She couldn't boil an egg.

There was a young lady called Perkins,
Exceedingly fond of small gherkins;
She went out to tea,
And ate forty-three,
Which pickled her internal werkins.

Food Lymerics

There was a young man from Bengal
Who went to a fancy dress ball.
He went just for fun
Dressed up as a bun
And a dog ate him up in the hall!

GERARD BENSON

Yum!

I like pepper on my ice cream;
Some like ice cream chilly.
I put ice cubes in the tea pot;
Boiling tea is silly.

If you want your bread to harden,
(Hard enough to chew)
Mix the flour with best cement
And butter it with glue.

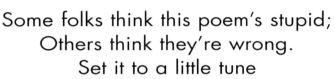

Some folks think this poem's stupid;
Others think they're wrong.
Set it to a little tune
And sing it as a song.

FOOD JOKES

whoops

argh....

he's nuts

Why did the beetroot blush?
It saw the salad dressing.

Which nut doesn't have a shell?
A doughnut!

How do you make a sausage roll?
Push it down the hill.

er

argh

What's the name for a train full of sweets?
A chew chew.

'Waiter, waiter, do you serve fish?'
'Yes, take a seat, Madam, we serve anybody.'

What do you call a stolen fish dinner?
Poached salmon.

chew chew

KIT WRIGHT

Greedyguts

I sat in the café and sipped at a coke.
There sat down beside me a WHOPPING great bloke
Who sighed as he elbowed me into the wall:
'Your trouble, my boy, is your belly's too small!
Your bottom's too thin! Take a lesson from me:
I may not be nice, but I'm GREAT, you'll agree,
And I've lasted a lifetime by playing this hunch:
The bigger the breakfast, the larger the lunch!

The larger the lunch, then the huger the supper.
The deeper the teapot, the vaster the cupper.
The fatter the sausage, the fuller the tea.
The more on the table, the BETTER FOR ME!'

His elbows moved in and his elbows moved out,
His belly grew bigger, chins wobbled about,
As forkful by forkful and plate after plate,
He ate and he ate and he ate and he ATE!

I hardly could breathe, I was squashed
out of shape,
So under the table I made my escape.
'Aha!' he rejoiced, 'when it's put
to the test,
The fellow who's fattest will
come off the best!
Remember, my boy, when
it comes to the crunch:
The bigger the breakfast,
the larger the lunch!

The larger the lunch, then the huger the supper.
The deeper the teapot the vaster the cupper.
The fatter the sausage, the fuller the tea.
The MORE on the table, the BETTER FOR ME!'

A lady came by who was scrubbing the floor
With a mop and a bucket. To even the score,
I lifted that bucket of water and said,
As I poured the whole lot of it over his head:

'I've found all my life, it's a pretty sure bet:
The FULLER the bucket, the WETTER you GET!'

DAVID HENRY WILSON

The Girl Who Didn't Believe in Ghosts

Cathy Tumbleweed knew everything. She knew that the earth was nearly 25,000 miles round and nearly 8,000 miles across; she knew that it was 238,854 miles away from the moon and nearly 93 million miles away from the sun; she knew that there were about 16,000 million people on the earth, and she knew that none of them was as clever as Cathy Tumbleweed. The other children in Miss Arnold's class knew that Cathy knew all these things, because whenever anybody told her anything she would immediately say: 'I know'. It's true that Cathy didn't always put her hand up when Miss Arnold asked a question, and it's also true that she made quite a lot of mistakes in her adds, her take aways, her stories and her comprehensions, but she would simply say: 'I knew it really', or 'I couldn't be bothered', and nobody could *prove* that she wasn't telling the truth.

Every so often Miss Arnold would read to the class from a story

book, and then there would be a discussion about it. On the day
that we're concerned with, she read them a ghost story – all about
a creaky old house which was inhabited by a creaky old man who
was one day visited by a very creaky, very old ghost who said he
was really the creaky old man himself as he would be in a few
creaky years' time. The children enjoyed the story – especially
all the creaky bits – and afterwards Miss Arnold asked them what
they knew about ghosts. Of course Cathy Tumbleweed knew
everything about ghosts, and so she put up her hand.

'Yes, Cathy?' said Miss Arnold.

'Ghosts,' said Cathy, 'don't exist. They are pigments of people's
imagination.'

'You mean figments,' said Miss Arnold.

'I know,' said Cathy.

'Well how do you know they don't exist?' asked Miss Arnold.

'Because,' said Cathy, 'it's a fact, and nobody's ever seen one.'

'Some people say they have,' said Miss Arnold.

'Well they can't *prove* it,' said Cathy. 'Nobody's ever *proved* it. If
they can't *prove* it, it's not true.'

Jonathan Justin James pointed out that nobody had ever *proved*
that ghosts *didn't* exist, Melvin Woolaway said he'd seen lots of
ghosts on television once, Gary Gillbank said he'd seen a ghost
once in a circus, Cathy said that was just someone dressed up as

a ghost . . . and so they went on and on till the bell rang and put an end to what Miss Arnold could only call a spirited discussion.

But that night the spirited discussion was to continue, for as soon as Cathy Tumbleweed's head came to rest on her pillow . . .

Creak. Crrrrrreak. Her bedroom door slowly grinds open, and in the darkness she sees a strange white shape floating towards the bed. The air is cold and clammy, like the hand of an ice-cream salesman, and Cathy shivers beneath her cover.

'Hello, Cathy Tumbleweed,' says a thin, whining voice.

'Who . . . who . . . who are you?' asks Cathy.

'Don't you know?' says the voice.

'N . . . n . . . no,' says Cathy.

'Ugh, I thought you knew everything,' says the ghost. 'I'm one of those things you don't believe in. I've come to *prove* I'm here.'

'I . . . I can s . . . see you're here,' says Cathy.

'I know,' says the ghost. 'Now listen to me. According to you, ghosts are figments of the imagination, aren't they?'

'Pigments,' says Cathy.

'Figments!' howls the ghost. 'Don't you know anything?! Now if I'm a figment of your imagination, why are you afraid of me?'

'I don't know!' says Cathy, shivering so hard that even her bed begins to creak.

88

'According to you nobody's ever seen a ghost. But you're seeing a ghost, aren't you?'

'Y . . . y . . . yes, I am.'

'Can you *prove* it?'

'Yes . . . no . . . no . . . yes.'

'That,' says the ghost, 'hardly answers my question. When you go to school tomorrow, will you be able to prove to everyone that you saw a ghost?'

'N . . . no,' says Cathy.

'Ha ha, ho ho,' says the ghost, 'but according to you, if you can't prove it, it's not true. Ha ha, ho ho!'

So saying, the ghost sits down on the bed and puts its hand on Cathy's cheek. Imagine a slug crawling over your face, or someone slapping you with a wet sock, or putting your head through a thick, damp cobweb, and you'll have some idea of the feeling Cathy had when the ghost put its hand on her cheek.

'Are you sure I'm here?' asks the ghost.

'Y . . . y . . . yes,' says Cathy. 'I can see you and feel you.'

'But no one at school has seen me or felt me!' says the ghost.

So saying, the ghost stands up and blows into Cathy's face. Imagine the smell of a cowshed that hasn't been cleaned for a week, or a piece of cheese left in the sun for a month, or the feet of an army after a ten-hour march, and you'll have some idea of the smell Cathy smelt when the ghost blew into her face.

'Are you positive I'm here?' asks the ghost.

'Y . . . y . . . yes,' says Cathy. 'I can see you and feel you and . . . ugh ugh . . . smell you!'

'But no one at school has seen me or felt me or . . . ugh ugh . . . smelt me,' says the ghost. 'And so, Cathy Tumbleweed, how can you prove that I was here?'

'But you *are* here,' wails Cathy.

'You know I'm here,' says the ghost, 'and I know I'm here. But how will *they* know I was here?'

'I don't know!' says Cathy. 'I don't know I don't know I don't know!'

'Aha!' says the ghost, in a voice that's just a little bit softer and a little bit friendlier. 'Now that's quite a good answer.'

'Is it?' says Cathy.

'Yes, it is,' says the ghost. 'Now let's see if you can tell me the answers to these questions. If it's half-past seven here, what's the time in New Zealand?'

'I . . . I don't know,' says Cathy.

'You don't know,' says the ghost. 'How tall is Mount Kilimanjaro?'

'I don't know,' says Cathy.

'You don't know,' says the ghost. 'How hot is the sun?'

'I don't know,' says Cathy.

'You don't know,' says the ghost. 'Good. That's what I like to hear. Now shall I tell you something, Cathy Tumbleweed?'

'Y . . . yes, please,' says Cathy.

'Well,' says the ghost, 'I don't know either! Ha ha, ho ho, hi hi, I don't know either!'

And the ghost laughs so loud and so long that Cathy starts laughing herself.

'Then why did you ask me?' giggles Cathy.

'Just to show you,' giggles the ghost, 'that nobody knows everything.'

And now the ghost stops giggling, and Cathy stops too, because not knowing things is really quite a serious business.

'You see,' says the ghost, 'none of us can be expected to know everything. And if we don't know something, it's best to admit it straight out. Then if we're lucky, someone might tell us the answer, or if we're clever we might find it out for ourselves. Now here's another question for you. What is tumbleweed?'

'I don't know,' says Cathy, confidently.

'Good,' says the ghost. 'That's a sensible answer. Well, tumbleweed is a plant that curls itself up into a ball and rolls around. And if you're going to get up in time for school tomorrow, I suggest you curl yourself up in a little ball right now, and roll yourself to sleep.'

And that's just what Cathy did.

Cathy has really changed a lot since her meeting with the ghost, and she's learnt a lot too, because she's always asking intelligent questions. Miss Arnold is very pleased with her, and so are Mr and Mrs Tumbleweed, though they're a little puzzled by her sudden passionate interest in ghost stories.

'It's just one of these phases,' said Mrs Tumbleweed one day. 'Children always go through them.'

'I know,' said Mr Tumbleweed.

Oh no you don't, thought Cathy, but she didn't say it out loud. After all, grown-ups can't know everything, but sometimes it's best not to tell them so.

RAYMOND WILSON
Happy Ghost

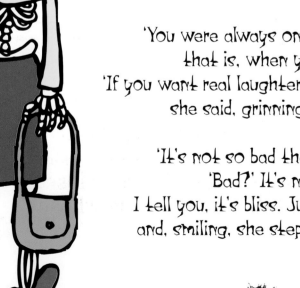

Joy Brightwell stood at my bedside
and my heart seized up with fear.
'Joy Brightwell,' I said, 'don't you know you're dead
and there's no way you should be here?'

'I thought I'd come back and take a look
at how it used to be,'
Joy Brightwell said, 'but the whole place is dead –
not to mention the company.'

'You were always one for a laugh, Joy –
that is, when you were here.'
'If you want real laughter, just try the Hereafter,'
she said, grinning from ear to ear.

'It's not so bad then, where you are?'
'Bad?' It's not bad at all.
I tell you, it's bliss. Just you try doing this!'
and, smiling, she stepped through the wall.

X. J. KENNEDY

Whose Boo is Whose?

Two ghosts I know once traded heads
And shrieked and shook their sheets to shreds –
'You're me!' yelled one, 'and me, I'm you.'
Now who can boo the loudest boo?'

'Me!' cried the other and for proof
He booed a boo that scared the roof
Right off our house. Our TV set
Jumped higher than a jumbo jet.

The first ghost snickered. 'Why, you creep,
Call that a boo? That feeble beep?
Hear *this*!' – and sucking in a blast
Of wind, he puffed his sheet so vast

And booed so hard, a passing goose
Lost all its down. The moon shook loose
And fell and smashed to smithereens –
Stars scattered like spilled jellybeans.

'How's that for booing, boy? I win,'
Said one. The other scratched a chin
Where only bone was – 'Win or lose?
How can we tell whose boo is whose?'

Why are cemeteries **SO** popular?

Who knows, but people are **dying** to get into them!

GHOST JOKES

1st Ghost: I've just bought a haunted bicycle.

2nd Ghost: How do you know it's haunted?

1st Ghost: There are spooks in the wheels.

What do you call a ghost doctor? A surgical spirit.

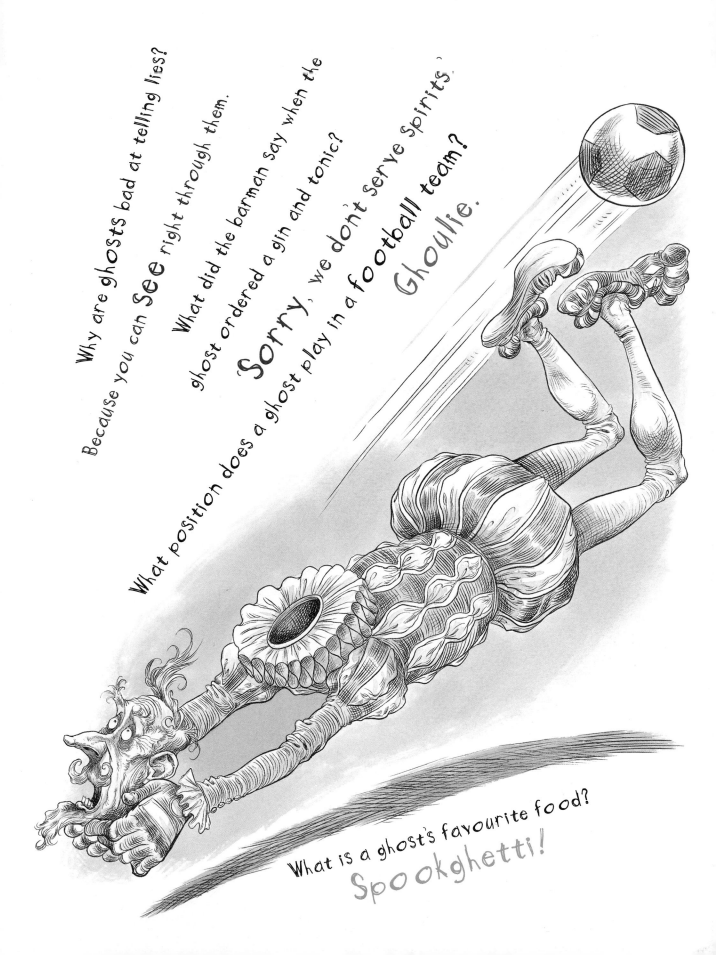

Why are ghosts bad at telling lies?

Because you can see right through them.

What did the barman say when the ghost ordered a gin and tonic?

'Sorry, we don't serve spirits.'

What position does a ghost play in a football team?

Ghoulie.

What is a ghost's favourite food?

Spookghetti!

COLONEL FAZACKERLEY

Colonel Fazackerley Butterworth-Toast
Bought an old castle complete with a ghost,
But someone or other forgot to declare
To Colonel Fazack that the spectre was there.

On the very first evening, while waiting to dine,
The Colonel was taking a fine sherry wine,
When the ghost, with a furious flash and a flare,
Shot out of the chimney and shivered, 'Beware!'

Colonel Fazackerley put down his glass
And said, 'My dear fellow, that's really first class!
I just can't conceive how you do it at all.
I imagine you're going to a Fancy Dress Ball?'

At this, the dread ghost gave a withering cry.
Said the Colonel (his monocle firm in his eye),
'Now just how you do it I wish I could think.
Do sit down and tell me, and please have a drink.'

The ghost in his phosphorous cloak gave a roar.
And floated about between ceiling and floor.
He walked through a wall and returned through a pane
And backed up the chimney and came down again.

Said the Colonel, 'With laughter I'm feeling quite weak!'
(As trickles of merriment ran down his cheek).
'My house-warming party I hope you won't spurn.
You *must* say you'll come and you'll give us a turn!'

At this, the poor spectre - quite out of his wits -
Proceeded to shake himself almost to bits.
He rattled his chains and he clattered his bones
And he filled the whole castle with mumbles and
moans.

But Colonel Fazackerley, just as before,
Was simply delighted and called out, 'Encore!'
At which the ghost vanished, his efforts in vain,
And never was seen at the castle again.

'Oh dear, what a pity!' said Colonel Fazack.
'I don't know his name, so I can't call him back.'
And then with a smile that was hard to define,
Colonel Fazackerley went in to dine.

CHRISTIAN MORGENSTERN
The Handkerchief Ghost

There is a ghost
That eats handkerchiefs;
It keeps you company
On all your travels, and
Eats your handkerchiefs
Out of your trunk, your
Bed, your washstand,
Like a bird eating
Out of your hand, – not
All of them and not
All at one go. With
Eighteen handkerchiefs
You set out, a proud mariner,
On the seas of the Unknown;
With eight or perhaps
Seven you come back, the
Despair of the housewife.

BARBARA IRESON

The Small Ghostie

When it's late and it's dark
And everyone sleeps . . . shh shh shh,
Into our kitchen
A small ghostie creeps . . . shh shh shh.

We hear knocking and raps
And then rattles and taps,

Then he clatters and clangs
And he batters and bangs,

And he whistles and yowls
And he screeches and howls . . .

So we pull up our covers over our heads
And we block up our ears and
WE STAY IN OUR BEDS.

JOHN HEATH-STUBBS

The Ghost of Gruesome Towers

I am the ghost of Gruesome Towers –
I haunt there, in nocturnal hours,
And do it rather well, because
This talent is, and always was
A kind of speciality
In our distinguished family.

My grandad was a hideous Ghoul
Who came, I'm told, from Istanbul,
His wife, the Lady Hypermania,
A vampiress from Transylvania.
Her story has a tragic twist –
An interfering exorcist
Destroyed in – I have to say –
A most ungentlemanly way.
He staked her through the heart –
to boot,
He stuffed her full of garlic-root.

My auntie is a Bleeding Nun –
I'm told she gets a lot of fun
Through haunting a monastic grange.
She has a quite surprising range
Of gibberings, and sepulchral groans,
Weird wailings, and despairing moans.

My uncle Poltergeist, whose haunt
Is a posh West End restaurant,
Has lately gained a lot of clout
Through throwing pots and pans about -
Sieves, cullenders and nutmeg-graters.
The affluent diners and the waiters
See knives and forks and tableware
Go madly hurtling through the air -
He once hurled a whole dinner service
At Lady Aspidistra Purvis.

My nephew - who's a bright young spark,
And just about to make his mark
(For to go far he has been tipped)
Haunts a damp, gloomy, Gothic crypt.
He's slowly mastering the technique
Of the high-pitched bloodcurdling shriek.
He's just a Nameless Something now,
But soon he'll learn his trade - and how!

I know what you're about to say -
This haunting lark has had its day.
It's all a lot of foolish flummery,
Pretentious and outmoded mummery.
You think I'll never frighten you:
Well just you listen -

"Hoo! Hoo!! Hoo!!!"

ANONYMOUS

The Ghost and the Skeleton

A skeleton once in Khartoum
Invited a ghost to his room.
They spent the whole night
In the eeriest fight
As to who should be frightened of whom.

RAAAGH!

JANIS PRIESTLEY

I'm Not Scared of Ghosts

I'm not, really, I'm not.
It's the things that they drop
with a very loud thump
that give me a shock
and make me jump.
But I'm not scared of ghosts –
No, I'm N ... O ... t!

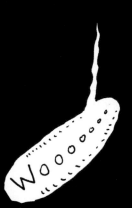

Woooo

TERRY JONES
The Sea Tiger

There was once a tiger who told the most enormous lies. No matter how hard he tried, he just couldn't tell the truth.

Once the monkey asked the tiger where he was going. The tiger replied that he was on his way to the moon, where he kept a store of tiger-cheese which made his eyes brighter than the sun so that he could see in the dark. But in fact he was going behind a bush for a snooze.

Another time, the snake asked the tiger round for lunch, but the tiger said that he couldn't come because a man had heard him singing in the jungle, and had asked him to go to the big city that very afternoon to sing in the opera.

'Oh!' said the snake. 'Before you go, won't you sing something for me?'

'Ah no,' said the tiger, 'if I sing before I've had my breakfast, my tail swells up and turns into a sausage, and I get followed around by sausage-flies all day.'

*

One day, all the animals in the jungle held a meeting, and decided they'd cure the tiger of telling such enormous lies. So they sent the monkey off to find the wizard who lives in the snow-capped mountains. The monkey climbed for seven days and seven nights, and he got higher and higher until at last he reached the cave in the snow where the wizard lived.

At the entrance to the cave he called out: 'Old wizard, are you there?'

And a voice called out: 'Come in, monkey, I've been expecting you.'

So the monkey went into the cave. He found the wizard busy preparing spells, and he told him that the animals of the jungle wanted to cure the tiger of telling such enormous lies.

'Very well,' said the wizard. 'Take this potion, and pour it into the tiger's ears when he is asleep.'

'But what will it do, wizard?' asked the monkey.

The wizard smiled and said: 'Rest assured, once you've given him this potion, everything the tiger says will be true all right.'

So the monkey took the potion and went back to the jungle where he told the other animals what they had to do.

That day, while the tiger was having his usual nap behind the bush, all the other animals gathered around in a circle and the monkey crept up very cautiously to the tiger and carefully poured a little of

the potion into first one of the tiger's ears and then into the other. Then he ran back to the other animals, and they all called out: 'Tiger! Tiger! Wake up, tiger!'

After a while, the tiger opened one eye, and then the other. He was a bit surprised to find all the other animals of the jungle standing around him in a circle.

'Have you been asleep?' asked the lion.

'Oh no,' said the tiger, 'I was just lying here, planning my next expedition to the bottom of the ocean.'

When they heard this, all the other animals shook their heads and said: 'The wizard's potion hasn't worked. Tiger's still telling us whopping lies as ever!'

But just then the tiger found himself leaping to his feet and bounding across the jungle. 'But it's true!' he cried to his own surprise.

'What are you doing, tiger?' they asked.

'I'm going to fly there!' he called and, sure enough, he spread out his legs and soared up high above the trees and across the top of the jungle.

Now if there's one thing tigers don't like, it's heights, and so the tiger yelled out: 'Help! I *am* flying! Get me down!'

But he found himself flying on and on until the jungle was far behind him and he flew over the snow-capped mountains where the wizard lived. The wizard looked up at the tiger flying overhead and smiled to himself and said: 'Ha-ha, old tiger, you'll always tell the truth now. For anything you say will become true – even if it wasn't before!'

And the tiger flew on and on, and he got colder and colder and, if there's one thing tigers hate worse than heights, it's being cold.

At length, he found himself flying out over the sea, and then suddenly he dropped like a stone, until he came down splash in the middle of the ocean. Now if there's one thing that tigers hate more than heights and cold, it's getting wet.

'Urrrrgh!' said the tiger, but down and down he sank, right to the bottom of the ocean, and all the fish came up to him and stared, so he chased them off with his tail.

Then he looked up and he could see the bottom of the waves high above him, and he swam up and up, and just as he was running out of breath he reached the surface. Then he struggled and splashed and tried to swim for the shore.

Just then a fishing boat came by, and all the fishermen gasped in amazement to see a tiger swimming in the middle

of the ocean. Then one of them laughed and pointed at the tiger and said: 'Look! A sea tiger!'

And they all laughed and pointed at the tiger, and, if there's one thing tigers hate worse than heights and cold and getting wet, it's being laughed at.

The poor tiger paddled away as fast as he could, but it was a long way to the shore, and eventually the fishermen threw one of their nets over him and hauled him on to the boat.

'Oh ho!' they laughed. 'Now we can make a fortune by getting this sea tiger to perform tricks in the circus!'

Now this made the tiger really angry because, if there's one thing tigers hate more than heights and cold and getting wet and being laughed at, it's performing tricks in the circus. So as soon as they landed, he tore up the net, and leapt out of the boat, and ran home to the forest as fast as his legs would carry him.

And he never told any lies, *ever* again.

ANONYMOUS

Rabbit

A rabbit raced a turtle,
You know the turtle won;
And Mister Bunny came in late,
A little hot cross bun!

ANONYMOUS

Frog

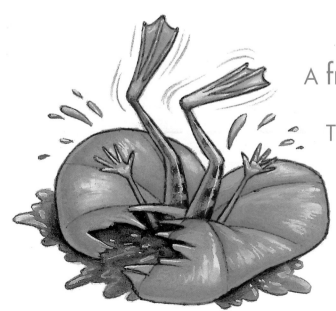

A froggie sat on a lily pad
Looking up at the sky:
The lily pad broke and the
frog fell in,
Water all in his eye.

JAMES REEVES

If Pigs
Could Fly

If pigs could fly, I'd fly a pig
To foreign countries small and big –
To Italy and Spain,
To Austria, where cowbells ring,
To Germany, where people sing –
And then come home again.

I'd see the Ganges and the Nile;
I'd visit Madagascar's isle,
And Persia and Peru.
People would say they'd never seen
So odd, so strange an air-machine
As that on which I flew.

Why, everyone would raise a shout
To see his trotters and his snout
Come floating from the sky;
And I would be a famous star
Well known in countries near and far –
If only pigs could fly!

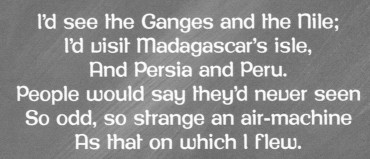

OGDEN NASH

The Octopus

Tell me, O Octopus, I begs,
Is those things arms, or is they legs?
I marvel at thee, Octopus;
If I were thou, I'd call me Us.

ANIMAL JOKES

Why did the **chicken** run on to the football pitch?
The referee called a **fowl**.

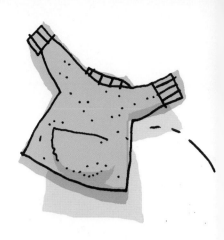

What do you get if you cross a **sheep** with a **kangaroo**?
A woolly jumper.

What do you give a sick **pig**?
Oinkment.

What do you get if you cross an **owl** with a **skunk**?
A bird that **smells** but doesn't give a hoot.

What does the **hedgehog** have for his lunch?
Prickled onions.

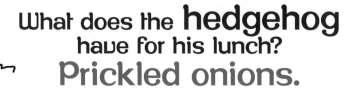

What do you get if you pour boiling water down a **rabbit** hole?

Hot cross **bunnies**.

A man went into a pet shop. 'Do you have any **dogs** going cheap?' 'No sir,' said the shopkeeper. 'All ours go "**bow-wow**".'

What is the difference between a **dog** and a **flea**? A dog can have fleas; a flea can't have dogs.

'Doctor, doctor, I keep thinking I'm a **dog**.'

'Lie down on this couch and I'll examine you.'

'I can't. I'm not allowed on the furniture.'

HILAIRE BELLOC

THE ELEPHANT

When people bear this beast to mind,
They marvel more and more
At such a LITTLE tail behind,
So **LARGE** a trunk before.

THE GECKO

DICK KING-SMITH

The GECKO has adhesive toes,
Straight up the wall the Gecko goes.
And then – and this is most appealing –
The Gecko walks across the ceiling!

Foolhardy is the one who tries
This topsy-turvy exercise.
To sudden death you will be fated –
The Gecko can't be imitated.

EDWARD LEAR
Calico Pie

Calico Pie,
The Little Birds fly
Down to the calico tree,
Their wings were blue,
And they sang 'Tilly-loo!'
Till away they flew, –

And they never came back to me!
They never came back!
They never came back!
They never came back to me!

Calico Jam,
The little Fish swam
Over the syllabub sea,
He took off his hat,
To the Sole and the Sprat,
And the Willeby-wat, –

But he never came back to me!
He never came back!
He never came back!
He never came back to me!

Calico Ban,
The little Mice ran,
To be ready in time for tea,
Flippity flup,
They drank it all up,
And danced in the cup, –

But they never came back to me!
They never came back!
They never came back!
They never came back to me!

Calico Drum,
The Grasshoppers come,
The Butterfly, Beetle, and Bee,
Over the ground,
Around and round,
With a hop and a bound, –

But they never came back!
They never came back!
They never came back!
They never came back to me!

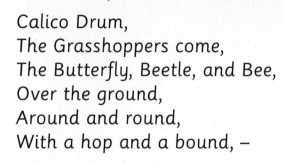

KIT WRIGHT
THE SYMPATHETIC RATS

York Minster was troubled with rats.
They were driving the Archbishop bats.
(One daredevil blighter
Ran right down his mitre
And bit a chunk out of his spats!)

So he said to the Dean
'Well, I just about *died*!
What on earth can we do?'
And the Dean, he replied:

'I'm getting a firm in from Kidderminster
Who really *do* know how to ridderminster
Of all kinds of pest.
They're the tops, they're the best!
But they charge about five thousand
quidderminster.

'That's quite a big chunk
Of episcopal dough
And how we shall raise it
I really don't know.'

Then the Archbishop broke down and cried.
The sight *put the rats on his side*!
They held a tombola
And raised the payola
And paid for the poison – and died!

ANONYMOUS

If You Should Meet A Crocodile

If you should meet a crocodile,
Don't take a stick and poke him;
Ignore the welcome in his smile,
Be careful not to stroke him.
For as he sleeps upon the Nile,
He thinner gets and thinner;
But whene'er you meet a crocodile
He's ready for his dinner.

ANIMAL JOKES

What type of **dog**
runs away from frying pans?
A **sausage** dog.

What happened to the **cat**
who swallowed a ball of wool?
She had **mittens**.

What's the
difference
between
a wet day
and a **lion**
with toothache?
One's pouring
with rain;
the other's
roaring
with pain.

Why do
birds
fly south
in the winter?
It's too far
to walk.

122

What do you call a **camel** with three humps?
Humphrey.

What did the baby **sardine** say when he saw a submarine?
Look, Mum – a tin of **people!**

What do you get if you cross a **cat** with a lemon?
A sour **puss.**

What card game do **crocodiles** like to play?
Snap.

ROGER McGOUGH
Bookworms

Bookworms
are the **cleverest**
of all the worms I know

While others
meet their fate
on a fisherman's hook as bait

Or churn out **silk**
or **chew** up earth
or simply burn and **glow**

They loll
about in libraries
eating **words** to make them grow

(**Vegetarians** mainly,
they are careful
what they eat

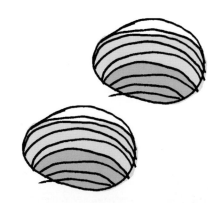

Avoiding names
of **animals**
or references to meat)

They live
to **ripe** old ages
and when it's time to wend

They **slip**
between the pages
curl up, and eat
'The End.'

INDEX

ACKNOWLEDGEMENTS

The publisher gratefully acknowledges the following for permission to reproduce copyright material in this anthology:

'Laughter Rap in Plastic Town' by John Agard from *Laughter Is an Egg* (Viking, 1990) copyright © John Agard 1990, reprinted by kind permission of the author c/o Caroline Sheldon Literary Agency; 'The Elephant' by Hilaire Belloc from *Cautionary Verses* (Random House) copyright © Estate of Hilaire Belloc 1940, reprinted by permission of The Peters, Fraser & Dunlop Group Limited on behalf of the author's estate; 'Yum!' by Gerard Benson from *Evidence of Elephants* (Viking, 1995) copyright © Gerard Benson 1995, reprinted by kind permission of the author c/o Campbell Thomson & McLaughlin Ltd; 'The Pudding like a Night on the Sea' by Ann Cameron from *The Julian Stories* (Victor Gollancz, 1982) copyright © Ann Cameron 1981, reprinted by permission of Penguin Books Ltd; 'Colonel Fazackerley' by Charles Causley from *Figgie Hobbin* (Macmillan, 1970) copyright © Charles Causley 1970, reprinted by kind permission of the author c/o David Higham Associates Ltd; 'My Dad the Headmaster' by Paul Cookson from *More Secret Lives of Teachers* (Macmillan, 1997) copyright © Paul Cookson 1997, reprinted by kind permission of the author; 'The Tummy Beast' by Roald Dahl from *Dirty Beasts* (Jonathan Cape Ltd, 1984) copyright © Roald Dahl Nominee Ltd 1983; 'Lost and Found' by Richard Edwards from *A Mouse in My Roof* (Orchard Books, 1988, a division of The Watts Publishing Group Limited, 96 Leonard Street, London EC2A 4XD) copyright © Richard Edwards 1988; 'Christmas Thank Yous' by Mick Gowar from *Swings and Roundabouts* (HarperCollins Publishers) copyright © Mick Gowar, reprinted by permission of HarperCollins Publishers Ltd; 'The Small Ghostie' by Barbara Ireson from *Rhyme Time II* (Beaver Books) copyright © Barbara Ireson, reprinted by kind permission of the author; 'The Sea Tiger' by Terry Jones from *Fairy Tales* (Pavilion Books, 1981), copyright © Terry Jones 1981, reprinted by permission of Pavilion Books; 'Whose Boo is Whose?' by X. J. Kennedy from *The Phantom Ice Cream Man* (Margaret K. McElderry Books, Atheneum Books for Young Readers, 1979) copyright © X. J. Kennedy 1979, reprinted by permission of Curtis Brown Ltd NY; 'The Gecko' by Dick King-Smith from *Alphabeasts* (Victor Gollancz, 1990) copyright © Dick King-Smith 1990, reprinted by permission of Fox Busters Ltd c/o A P Watt; 'Bookworms' by Roger McGough from *An Imaginary Menagerie* (Viking, 1988) copyright © Roger McGough 1988, reprinted by permission of The Peters Fraser and Dunlop Group Limited on behalf of the author; 'Fair Exchange' by Margaret Mahy from *Nonstop Nonsense* (J. M. Dent & Sons, 1977) copyright © Margaret Mahy 1977, reprinted by permission of Orion Children's Books; 'Unexpected Summer Soup' by Margaret Mahy from *The First Margaret Mahy Story Book* copyright © Margaret Mahy, published by permission of Orion Children's Books; 'The One That Got Away' by Jan Mark from *Story Chest: 100 Bedtime Stories* (Viking Kestrel, 1986) copyright © Jan Mark 1986, reprinted by permission of David Higham Associates Ltd; 'Granny' by Spike Milligan from *Silly Verse for Kids* (Puffin Books, 1968) copyright © Spike Milligan 1959, reprinted by permission of Spike Milligan Productions Ltd; 'Golden Syrup' by S-J Mortimer, copyright © S-J Mortimer 1999, reprinted by kind permission of the author; 'The Octopus' by Ogden Nash, first published in the UK in *Candy is Dandy: The Best of Ogden Nash*, reprinted by permission of Andre Deutsch Ltd, first published in the USA in *Verses From 1929 On* copyright © Ogden Nash 1942, first appeared in *The New Yorker*, reprinted by permission of Little Brown and Company (Inc.); 'Gust Becos I Cud Not Spel' by Brian Patten from *Gargling with Jelly* (Viking, 1985) copyright © Brian Patten 1985, reprinted by permission of Penguin Books Ltd; 'I'm not Scared of Ghosts' by Janis Priestley copyright © Janis Priestley, reproduced in association with Macmillan Children's Books, London; 'The Kwackagee' and 'If Pigs Could Fly' by James Reeves from *Complete Poems for Children* (Heinemann) copyright © James Reeves, reprinted by permission of the James Reeves Estate c/o Laura Cecil Literary Agency; 'Tricks' and 'Dracula Mask' by Michael Rosen from *Quick, Let's Get Out of Here* (Andre Deutsch, 1983) copyright © Michael Rosen 1983, reprinted by permission of Scholastic Children's Books; 'Auntie Meg's Cookery Book' by Vernon Scannell from *The Clever Potato* (Hutchinson) copyright © Vernon Scannell, reprinted by permission of Red Fox; 'In One Ear and Out the Other' by Colin West from *A Step in the Wrong Direction* (Hutchinson, 1984) copyright © Colin West 1984, reprinted by kind permission of the author; 'The Girl Who Didn't Belive in Ghosts' by David Henry Wilson from *The Fastest Gun Alive* (Chatto & Windus, 1978) copyright © David Henry Wilson 1978, reprinted by kind permission of the author; 'Happy Ghost' by Raymond Wilson from *To Be a Ghost* (Viking, 1991) copyright © Raymond Wilson 1991, reprinted by permission of Penguin Books Ltd; 'Greedyguts' by Kit Wright from *Hot Dog and Other Poems* (Kestrel, 1981) copyright © Kit Wright 1981, reprinted by permission of Penguin Books Ltd; 'The Sympathetic Rats' and 'What Went Wrong at my Sister's Wedding' by Kit Wright from *Great Snakes* (Viking, 1994) copyright © Kit Wright 1994, reprinted by permission of Penguin Books Ltd.